Monica stopped at her gate. "Good-bye," she said.

Rhoda went on. There was something sad about her. She looked lost as she walked up the road with the dark pines on either side. Monica wanted to say something more.

"Rhoda —" she called.

Rhoda stopped and looked back.

And then Monica could think of nothing to say — nothing except, "Last look!"

This was a game she had played when she was little. Whoever was the last person to look back lost the game. It was ridiculous, but she said it and turned quickly toward the house.

"Monica — wait!" called Rhoda. "Monica!" Her voice rose. "Help me! Help!*"*

Monica let herself into the house.

Her mother came out of the kitchen. "Who was screaming?"

"Rhoda," said Monica. "She was trying to make me look back."

"She was certainly trying hard," said her mother.

"She was, wasn't she?" said Monica. "She's really good at the game. She nearly made me look."

CLYDE ROBERT BULLA

PUFFIN BOOKS

PUFFIN BOOKS
Published by the Penguin Group
Penguin Books USA Inc., 375 Hudson Street, New York, New York 10014, U.S.A.
Penguin Books Ltd, 27 Wrights Lane, London W8 5TZ, England
Penguin Books Australia Ltd, Ringwood, Victoria, Australia
Penguin Books Canada Ltd, 10 Alcorn Avenue, Toronto, Ontario, Canada M4V 3B2
Penguin Books (N.Z.) Ltd, 182-190 Wairau Road, Auckland 10, New Zealand

Penguin Books Ltd, Registered Offices: Harmondsworth, Middlesex, England

First published in the United States of America by Thomas Y. Crowell, 1979
Published in Puffin Books, 1995

1 3 5 7 9 10 8 6 4 2

LIBRARY OF CONGRESS CATALOGING-IN-PUBLICATION DATA
Bulla, Clyde Robert.
Last look / Clyde Robert Bulla. p. cm.
Summary: Monica doesn't particularly like the new girl at school,
but when she receives a mysterious note stating that Rhoda
is in danger she must make a decision whether to help or not.
ISBN 0-14-036733-0
[1. Friendship—Fiction.] I. Title.
PZ7.B912Las 1995 [Fic]—dc20 94-38649 CIP AC

Printed in the United States of America

To J.D.

Contents

Rhoda

Monica was walking to school with her two best friends, Fran and Audrey. She was telling them about the surprising thing that had happened over the weekend. When she finished, they stopped in the middle of the road and stared at her.

Fran said, "I don't believe it!"

Audrey said, "Are you *sure?*"

"Diane told me herself," said Monica.

"But she was at school on Friday," said Fran. "Why didn't she tell us then?"

"She didn't know," said Monica. "She probably

didn't find out till Saturday. She called Madame Vere first, and then she called me."

"Why didn't she call the rest of us?" asked Fran.

"There wasn't time," said Monica. "Her father's company said, You have to go *now*, and that's the way it was."

"Life is so weird," said Audrey. "Friday she was at school. Now she's on her way to Switzerland, and we may never see her again."

"Ah, Switzerland!" said Fran. "All those lakes and mountains! I'd like to go there."

"I'd like it if it could be an adventure—maybe something like a secret mission," said Monica. "But just to take a trip, no. I'd rather be here."

They started walking again. Fran said suddenly, "I wonder who the new girl will be."

"There *will* be a new girl, won't there?" said Audrey.

"There always is," said Monica.

They were in their last year at Madame Vere's School. It was a summer school for girls from six to twelve. Madame's schoolhouse was her home, and she had room for no more than thirty pupils at a time. There was always a waiting list. When a girl dropped out or moved away, another was always waiting to take her place.

"It could be somebody little," said Fran. "Somebody in the first grade."

"I hope it's somebody older—about our age," said Audrey. "That would be more interesting."

They turned down a side road. They could see Madame's house ahead, with the tall white pillars that made it look like a Greek temple. Behind it was the lake, silver-blue and dazzling in the morning light.

They were almost late. They slipped into the study hall that was really Madame's living room. They took their places.

"Look!" whispered Fran. "She's here already!"

And there she was, in Diane's old place by the window—the new girl.

Madame was at her desk. Tiny Madame with her

dyed black hair and a dab of rouge on each cheekbone.

"Good morning," she said. "As some of you may know, one of our girls has left us. Diane and her family have gone to live in Switzerland. She asked me to tell you she enjoyed being in school with you, and she wished there'd been time to say good-bye."

Madame's shrewd, kindly eyes looked out at them all. "And now I'd like you to meet a new pupil. Will you stand please, Rhoda?"

The new girl stood. She was thin and fairly tall. Her short hair was blonde, but her eyebrows were dark. They almost met above the bridge of her nose. Her face was long and rather bony. She stood there, looking perfectly calm.

"Rhoda has come to spend the summer with her grandmother, Mrs. Gorman," said Madame Vere.

Fran gave Monica a look.

"Welcome to our school," said Madame Vere. "We hope you'll be happy here."

The new girl said, "Thank you." She glanced coolly about the room before she sat down.

At noon Monica, Fran, and Audrey took their lunch boxes to the shady side of the house.

"What do you think?" asked Audrey.

"She looks older than any of us," said Fran. "Don't you think so, Monica?"

"It may be her hair," Monica said. "That haircut makes her look sophisticated."

"Imagine spending the summer with *Mrs. Gorman,*" said Fran.

"Quiet!" Monica warned her.

Rhoda was coming toward them.

"Hello," she said. Her voice was a little louder than it needed to be. She sat down on the grass with them and opened her lunch box. It seemed to be empty except for an apple.

"What are your names?" she asked.

They told her.

"Are you summer people, or do you live here all year?" she asked.

"We're summer people," Monica answered. "Our families have cottages here on the lake."

"I guess not many people live here the year round. My grandmother is one of the few." Rhoda was watching their faces. "Do you know my grandmother?"

"We know who she is," said Fran.

"And where she lives," said Audrey. "Just up from the haunted house."

"You mean the empty house down by the lake?" Rhoda was still watching them. "Why do you call it a *haunted* house?"

Monica, Fran, and Audrey looked at one another. They began to laugh. "It's an old joke," said Audrey.

"It *looks* like a haunted house, don't you think?" said Fran.

"I don't know. I don't know how a haunted house is supposed to look." Rhoda bit into her apple with her long white teeth. Monica thought of a horse—she couldn't help it.

"I think you'll like our school," said Audrey. "Madame is a wonderful teacher. She goes all over the world, and she—well—she kind of brings the world to us."

Rhoda took another bite out of her apple. She said, "I'd like to join your club."

"What club?" asked Monica.

"The one you belong to."

"I don't belong to any."

"You mean you don't have a club—the three of you?"

"No. What made you think we did?"

"You keep together," said Rhoda. "When you came in this morning, I heard somebody say, 'There's the club.' "

"Somebody was being funny," said Monica.

"We're friends and we're together a lot, that's all. We live close together."

"Where?" asked Rhoda.

"Well—Fran and Audrey live side by side, just beyond Lake Drive. I live a little farther on. It's the white cottage with the blue tent in the yard."

"I saw that tent," said Rhoda. "What is it for?"

"I sleep in it," Monica told her.

"Why?"

"I just like to. It's nice out there under the trees."

"We all live in a row. That's good," said Rhoda. "We can all walk together."

For a little while no one spoke. Then Monica said slowly, "Yes—I suppose we can."

The Four

So the three became four. On the way to school, on the way home, they walked together.

Toward the middle of the week, Madame Vere took Monica aside and said, "I was afraid the new girl might be lonely, but everyone has made her welcome. That's partly because of you. You've always been one of our leaders, and for you and Rhoda to be friends—well—I know what it means to her."

"I'm not so sure we *are* friends," Monica started to say, but Madame gave her a pat and sent her away.

On the Friday of Rhoda's first week at school,

the four were walking home together.

"You hear about Lake Chester," Rhoda was saying, "and you think it's a city or at least a town. But it's just some houses strung along a lake. I don't think this place will ever get to be a town."

"I hope not," said Fran. "We like it the way it is."

"There's nothing much here," said Rhoda. "There's not even a theater."

"There's a movie theater over on The Point," said Audrey.

"I don't mean that. I mean a real one where they have plays." Rhoda sighed. "I miss the theater."

"I like the theater, too," said Monica. "When we're in New York, we go to some of the Broadway plays."

"Then you must have seen my mother," said Rhoda. "She's Elaine Boston."

"No, I don't think I have," said Monica. "I've heard her name, though."

"I should hope so. After her next play, she just may be the best-known actress in the country. We were in a play together once."

"You're an actress, too?" asked Audrey.

"I only had three lines." Rhoda laughed. "But I learned a lot. There's such excitement in the theater. I just may go on to be an actress."

"We have a school play every year," said Monica. "We make our own sets and costumes—"

"Not like Broadway, of course," said Fran.

She and Audrey stopped off at their houses. Monica and Rhoda went on together.

Rhoda said, "Why don't we plan something for the weekend? Let's have a picnic. We could ask Fran and Audrey if you wanted to, but I thought it might be fun for just the two of us."

"I can't," said Monica. "My father works in New Jersey, and he comes up every weekend. He and Mother and I always do something together when he's here."

"It doesn't matter," said Rhoda. "My mother may be coming up from New York anyway."

They had stopped in front of Monica's house. Monica's mother called from the doorway, "Telephone!"

Rhoda went on. Monica ran into the house.

Fran was on the telephone. "Can you come back here?" she asked. "We want to talk to you."

Monica walked back to Fran's. Fran and Audrey were waiting at the gate.

"How much longer is this going to go on?" asked Fran.

"What?" asked Monica.

"You know what," said Fran. "Every time we turn around, *she's* there."

"We used to have fun together," said Audrey. "Now we don't."

"Today was the worst." Fran held her nose and spoke in a loud singsong, " 'I miss the theater . . . I just may go on to be an actress.' "

"There *is* an Elaine Boston," said Monica. "I've heard of her."

"Do you think Rhoda was really in a Broadway play?" asked Fran.

"I suppose she could have been."

"If she was or if she wasn't, it's not important," Audrey spoke up. "The thing is, does she have to be with us every minute?"

"I'm not enjoying it any more than you are," said Monica, "but Madame is proud of the way we're being nice to the new girl. She told me so. Are we going to let her down?"

Fran said, after a moment, "We don't want to let Madame down. You know that. But do we have to let Rhoda push herself in wherever we go?"

"*I* don't know what to do," said Monica, "but things have a way of changing. Let's give it another week and see what happens."

Last Look

It was Monday again. The four were on their way to school.

Fran said to Monica, "I saw you go by with your father Saturday. He has a new car, hasn't he?"

"No, it's the same one. We went past The Point, and there was a carnival. We came back and picked up Mother, and we all went to it."

"We sailed over to the island," said Audrey. "You know the pretty beach with the big red rock? We had it all to ourselves."

"Mother and Daddy and I went riding yesterday," said Fran, "and if any of you go to the stables, don't let them give you a horse named Lightning. He won't move!"

Rhoda had been quiet. Monica asked her, "Did your mother come up from New York?"

"She phoned me instead," said Rhoda. "We talked an hour and a half. Listen, I've been thinking. Why don't we have a club? There could be just us at first. Later, if we wanted to, we could take in some others."

Monica felt Fran and Audrey looking at her. "What kind of club?" she asked.

"Just for getting together and—and having talks," said Rhoda.

"That's not much of a reason," said Monica.

"We could *think* of a reason."

No one answered, and they left it there.

After school Madame asked Rhoda to wait.

The other three were out on the front steps.

"Are we supposed to wait, too?" asked Audrey.

"Nobody told us to," said Fran. "She and Madame are in there talking. Let's go."

They started toward the highway.

"This is the way it used to be," said Audrey.

"And isn't it nice!" Fran was in the middle. She linked arms with Monica and Audrey.

"It *is* nice," said Monica, "but you can almost feel sorry for her sometimes."

"I don't feel sorry for her," said Fran. "Why is she always pushing herself in where she's not wanted? Why is she always giving herself airs? The tales she tells—you *know* they aren't true. Like her mother calling and talking an hour and a half—*that* never happened."

"How do you know?" asked Monica.

"Because her grandmother doesn't have a telephone. We know Elmo, the telephone serviceman, and he says old Mrs. Gorman won't have one."

"I thought everybody had a telephone," said Audrey.

"Not Mrs. Gorman. She won't have one. She won't fix up her house either. It looks worse than the haunted house."

Audrey gave a moan. "Don't look now, but—"

Rhoda was running after them. "Wait!"

She caught up with them. She was waving a magazine. "Madame wanted to give me this. There's a picture of my mother on page twenty-four."

They looked at it. It wasn't much of a picture—a small, dim face among other faces—but the name was below for all to see: Elaine Boston.

"You can't tell much from this," said Rhoda. "I have some really good pictures I'll show you."

No one answered.

They came to Audrey's, then to Fran's.

As Fran started up the walk, Monica called after her, "Watch out for the bears!"

Fran looked toward her. "What—?"

"Last look!" said Monica and turned her head.

"Monica!" called Fran. "I forgot to tell you something. Monica—!"

Without stopping or looking back, Monica hurried on down the road.

"What was *that* all about?" asked Rhoda in a bewildered voice. She was running along beside Monica.

Monica was laughing. "It's a game. Didn't you ever play it?"

"Never!"

"When Fran left us just now, I made her look back, and I said, 'Last look.' Then she tried to make me look at her so *she* could say it. But I wouldn't look, so I won the game."

"It sounds like something little children would play."

"It is. We played it all the time when we were little. We're too old for it now, but sometimes something comes over us—"

"I suppose you always win," said Rhoda.

"Oh, no. I took her by surprise that time. Next time she'll probably surprise me."

Beauty and the Beast

It was time to talk about the school play. Madame Vere had called a meeting in the study hall.

"We're doing *Beauty and the Beast,*" she said. "We'll need actors, stagehands, and people to make sets and costumes. Let me know what you'd like to do. There's work for everyone."

"Who will the actors be?" someone asked.

"That's what we always think of first, isn't it?" said Madame Vere. "We'll need a Beauty and a Beast, of course. Then we'll need Beauty's sisters.

Let's take Beauty first. Do you have any ideas?"

"Monica," said one of the smaller girls, "because she's the prettiest."

Others took it up. There was a chorus of "Monica!"

Madame looked pleased. "A good choice. Monica, will you take the part?"

Monica's cheeks were pink. "If—if you want me," she said.

"Now," said Madame Vere, "the next part—"

Someone broke in. "May I say something?"

It was Rhoda.

"Beauty is the only part in the play worth having," she said. "Do you think it's fair just to hand it out without giving anyone else a chance?"

The room grew still.

"The part wasn't just handed out," said Madame Vere. "It seems to me that Monica was chosen by the school."

"Excuse me for saying so," said Rhoda, "but that's not a very good way to cast a part. The best way is to try out for it."

Madame Vere looked thoughtful. "Very well," she said. "Who wants to try out?"

Rhoda's hand went up.

"Who else?" asked Madame. There were no other hands. "Of course, you're trying out, Monica."

"I'd rather not," said Monica.

"I understand how you feel," said Madame Vere, "but others in the school would like to see you in the part. Don't you think you owe it to them to try for it?"

Monica didn't answer.

"Shall we have the tryouts now," asked Madame Vere, "or do you want time to study the part?"

"I'm ready now," said Rhoda.

"And you, Monica?"

"Yes," said Monica.

She went up to the desk and stood beside Rhoda.

Madame Vere opened a book. "Here's something from Act Two. Who wants to read first?"

Rhoda took the book. She read in a loud, clear voice: "This castle is lovely to the sight, yet how I wish myself at home! Each night I weep, not knowing what may come tomorrow. All is strange here, even the bird calls . . . Hark! What was that?"

"Thank you," said Madame Vere. "Monica, please."

Monica read the lines. She read them badly, she thought. Twice she stumbled over words.

Madame thanked her. "How many feel that Rhoda should play the part? Raise your hands."

No hands were raised.

"How many feel that Monica should play it?"

There was a burst of applause. Hands went up all over the room.

Madame Vere said to Rhoda and Monica, "Thank you. You may take your seats."

As they sat down, Monica heard a whisper, "Rhoda could be the Beast!"

If Rhoda heard, she gave no sign. She looked calm. She was even smiling.

"Since this *is* a girls' school," Madame was saying, "some of you will be playing boys' parts. Would anyone like to try out for the Beast? It's a good part, too . . . No? Then we'll talk about it and try to make a choice."

The meeting went on.

"We'd like you to have a part, Rhoda," said Madame Vere.

"Couldn't I work on the sets?" asked Rhoda.

"Of course, if you'd rather. I'll put you down for that."

After school the four started home together.

Rhoda said to Monica, "Congratulations, Beauty."

"Thank you," said Monica. "You read better than I did. You should have got the part."

Rhoda's mouth curled. "You don't think I *wanted* it?"

"You mean you *didn't* want it?" asked Fran.

"Certainly not."

"Then why did you pretend you did? You made things awkward for everyone."

"I was teaching Madame a lesson," said Rhoda. "She was going to hand the part to Monica on a silver platter. I was letting her know things aren't done that way."

"Things *are* done that way. In our school they are," said Fran. "We talk about the parts and who might be best for them. Then we sort of vote on it. This isn't a Broadway theater. It's a little play in a little school."

They walked along without saying anything, without looking at one another. Audrey turned off at her house. Fran turned off at hers. Monica and Rhoda went on together.

Monica tried to start a conversation. Rhoda hardly answered. She seemed to be deep in her own thoughts.

Monica stopped at her gate. "Good-bye," she said.

"What?" said Rhoda.

"I live here, remember? I said good-bye."

"Oh. Good-bye." Rhoda went on.

There was something sad about her. She looked lost as she walked up the road with the dark pines on either side.

Monica wanted to say something more.

"Rhoda—" she called.

Rhoda stopped and looked back.

And then Monica could think of nothing to say —nothing except, "Last look!"

It was ridiculous, but she said it and turned quickly toward the house.

"Monica—wait!" called Rhoda. "Monica!" Her voice rose. "Help me! *Help!*"

Monica let herself into the house.

Her mother came out of the kitchen. "Who was screaming?"

"Rhoda," said Monica. "She was trying to make me look back."

"She was certainly trying hard," said her mother.

"She was, wasn't she?" said Monica. "She's really good at the game. She nearly made me look."

"Tell No One"

The next day was Saturday, and Monica slept late. She was barely awake when a car pulled up beside her tent.

She opened the flap. "Father!"

He slid out of the car—a long-legged man in jacket and jeans.

"You must have left New Jersey in the middle of the night," she said.

"Just about." He grinned at her. "Still sleeping in that tent, I see, when you have a perfectly good bedroom."

"You don't know how nice it is out here," she said.

"And I may never find out, as long as I have a roof to sleep under. Come on. Get dressed. We're going out for breakfast."

They had breakfast at a pancake house on The Cove—Father, Mother, and Monica. They drove all the way around the lake.

It was noon when they came back to the cottage. There was a woman at the gate. She wore an odd-looking brown dress—long in front, short in the back—and her hair was gray and wild. She half waved as they drove in.

"It's Rhoda's grandmother!" said Monica. "I'll go see what she wants."

She ran out to the gate. "Hello, Mrs. Gorman," she said.

The woman looked ill. Her skin was blotchy. She put a hand to her face as if the light hurt her eyes.

"Are you Monica?" she asked in a hoarse, deep voice.

"Yes, I am."

"Is she—is my granddaughter here?"

"Rhoda? No, she isn't."

"She didn't come home with you yesterday?"

"No."

"Well, then—" Mrs. Gorman smiled. It was a ghastly smile. "It's all right, dear. I understand now. Thank you so much."

She was on her way up the road.

Monica ran after her. "Do you mean Rhoda didn't come home from school yesterday?"

"Well, yes—I suppose she did. But I never saw her. Sometimes I'm in the back of the house, and I don't always—" The woman smiled again. "It's all right."

"If you haven't seen her, how can you say it's all right?"

"Oh, she went to her mother's. She went to New York."

"Without telling you?"

"She *did* tell me, in a way. She's not very nice to me, you know. Sometimes she's not nice at all. She's been saying she was going home to her mother's. She said she had her own money and she could take the bus, and that's what she's done."

"Are you sure?"

"Oh, yes. I'm sure now."

"And you're not worried?"

"No, no, and don't you be worried either. Good-bye, dear, and thank you."

Monica told her mother and father afterward, "She hasn't seen Rhoda since yesterday morning, and she doesn't see why anyone should worry. Do you think I should have told her about yesterday?"

"What about yesterday?" asked Mother.

"Don't you remember? About playing Last Look. Maybe Rhoda wasn't playing. Maybe she really saw something—"

"What could she have seen in the road in the middle of the afternoon?"

"You heard how she screamed. Maybe she *was* in danger."

"What kind of danger?" asked Father.

"I don't know."

"You don't know, but you're building up things in your mind. Here's how it looks to me," he said. "This Rhoda and her grandmother don't get on too well. The girl walked out and took a bus to her mother's. The grandmother thought she *might* have spent the night with you. When she found out Rhoda wasn't here, she knew the girl must be with her mother, so she stopped worrying. And you should stop, too."

Father left on Sunday night. The next morning Monica was walking to school with Fran and Audrey.

"This is like the old days," said Fran. "Just the three of us again."

"I think we've seen the last of Rhoda," said Audrey.

"Aren't you worried at all?" asked Monica.

"Why?" asked Fran. "She can take care of herself."

At school Monica told Madame what had happened.

"It may be nothing serious," said Madame. "I think Rhoda will soon be back with us. I know how much her mother wanted her to come to our school."

On the way home that afternoon, Monica asked Fran and Audrey, "If you hear anything about Rhoda, will you let me know?"

"What is there to hear?" asked Fran.

"I thought she might give one of us a call from New York," said Monica.

"She wouldn't call me," said Fran.

"Or me," said Audrey. "She might give you a call, although I doubt it."

"I wish she would. Then I'd feel better," said Monica.

But there was no call from New York. She really hadn't expected one.

It was a quiet evening. She did her homework. At half past nine she said good night to her mother and went out to the tent. The night was dark, and she found her way with a flashlight.

She lay in her sleeping bag. She listened to the wind for a long time before she went to sleep.

Something wakened her. It was a rustling sound. Not the wind. The wind had died, and the night was still.

She saw the clock on the ground beside her, its face glowing in the dark. Two o'clock.

She found the flashlight and turned it on. In its beam she saw something stuck in the tent flap. A piece of paper.

She took out the paper. There were words on it —words made up of letters cut from a newspaper.

Monica. Tell no one. Rhoda in danger. Go to haunted house Tuesday at midnight. Receive message. Go alone. Tell no one.

The Sheriff

Monica felt her way through the dark house. She couldn't remember how she had gotten there. She found the door of her mother's bedroom.

"Mother—"

The light came on. Mother sat up in bed.

"What is it?"

The paper shook in Monica's hand. "This was in my tent."

Mother took the note. "What on earth—!"

"I heard a sound," said Monica. "I think it was someone slipping the paper into the tent."

Mother read aloud, " 'Rhoda in danger.' "

"We have to call the police."

"Monica, I don't understand this. Could it be a joke?"

"A *joke?*"

"Maybe one of your friends—"

"No!"

Mother got out of bed. "I suppose I'd better call Hal."

Hal Ericson was the sheriff. He lived a mile down the road.

Mother called him. He was there in half an hour. He was a big man with thick white hair and pale blue eyes. He looked sleepy, and he looked bored.

He read the note. "Who is Rhoda?"

"Mrs. Gorman's granddaughter," Monica told him.

"Oh, yes. And her mother is an actress in New York. I used to know her name. Elaine—"

"Elaine Boston," said Monica.

"What about the girl?" asked the sheriff. "When did you last see her?"

"Friday, after school. She walked home with me. We were playing Last Look—"

"What's that?"

"A game. It's a little like playing tag with your eyes. Rhoda looked at me, and I said, 'Last look.' Then she tried to make me look at her so *she* could say it. I wouldn't look, and she started screaming. I thought she was just playing the game, so I didn't turn around. And then—"

"Yes?"

"Her grandmother came over the next day. She wanted to know if Rhoda had stayed all night with me."

"Was she upset?"

Monica tried to remember. "She didn't seem to be. She said Rhoda must have taken the bus and gone back to her mother's."

"And you think that didn't happen?" asked the

sheriff. "You think she disappeared while you were playing your game?"

"She could have, couldn't she?"

He was reading the note again. " 'Go to haunted house.' Is that the old Fenwick place where nobody lives?"

"It must be," said Mother.

Hal Ericson frowned. "I don't like empty houses. They make mischief. Stories grow up around them. Mystery stories." He looked at Monica. "You like mystery stories, don't you?"

She looked at him without answering.

"Some of your friends like them, too, don't they?" He sat back in his chair. "I remember some little girls here on the lake. They thought it would be fun to play ghost and maybe start a few ghost stories. One night they went to the old Fenwick place. They had candles. They might have burned the place down, but that didn't bother them. They went through the house and played they were haunting it. Somebody saw the lights and called me. The little girls didn't get away fast enough, and I caught them. They looked pretty foolish, I can tell you. They said they were just having fun, and I told them the police had better things to do than go out in the middle of the night for nothing. I guess you don't remember those girls. Their names were Fran, Audrey, and Monica."

Her face had grown warm. "That was a long time ago."

"Right. A long time ago. I should hope you wouldn't do anything like that now." The sheriff got up. "Good night. Try to get some sleep."

Mother went with him to the door. She came back.

Monica had flung herself into a chair. "He didn't believe me. He didn't believe a word I was saying!"

"You'll have to admit the story does sound strange," said Mother.

"What's strange about it?"

"If Rhoda is in danger, why did the note come to you? Why didn't it go to her grandmother?"

"How should I know? All I know is you don't believe me either."

"I never said that."

"You don't have to say it. Just because of what happened years ago, you think it's some game I'm playing. I'm sorry I told the sheriff, and I wish I hadn't told you."

"Monica—"

"I should have gone to the haunted house without telling anybody. Maybe I'd have found out something."

"Monica, I'll be honest with you. The sheriff does think it looks like some kind of joke. But he took the note with him. He's going to look into it. He's going to see Mrs. Gorman. He even said he'd go around to check the old house."

"He's doing me a big favor, isn't he?" Monica's voice was bitter. "It may be a matter of life and death, and he thinks it's a joke."

"You're tired, and so am I," said Mother. "Go to bed."

"Out there?"

"No, in your bedroom. Good night."

At Mrs. Gorman's

Mother said the next morning, "You won't talk about this at school, will you?"

Monica shook her head.

"The sheriff wouldn't want you to. It's easy to say too much about a thing like this."

"I know." Monica added to herself, I said too much last night. I shouldn't have told anyone.

But it was hard to be quiet. She wanted to say to Fran and Audrey, Rhoda is missing. I think she's being held for ransom.

When Madame asked about Rhoda, Monica

could hardly keep from saying, She won't be in school today. She may be kidnapped.

Fran asked on the way home, "What's the *matter* with you?"

"Nothing," said Monica.

"You're a million miles away," said Audrey.

Fran said, "It's something about Rhoda, isn't it?"

"You had a fight," said Audrey, "and that's why she didn't come to school."

"We didn't have a fight, and I don't know why she didn't come to school."

"But it's *something* about Rhoda, isn't it?" said Fran.

"You may as well tell us," said Audrey, "because we'll find out."

They left her. She walked on.

She didn't stop at home. She walked up the road past the place where she had last seen Rhoda. The pine woods on either side looked dark and strange.

A little way beyond the woods was Mrs. Gorman's house. It was big and old and falling apart. With the broken windows in the attic, and the sagging porches and balconies, it looked more haunted than the haunted house.

Monica went to the front door and knocked.

There were dragging footsteps inside. There was a crash, as if a chair had been knocked over. The door opened, and Mrs. Gorman peered out.

"Who are you?" she asked. "What do you want?"

"Don't you know me?" asked Monica. "You came to see me. You came to ask about Rhoda."

"Oh—yes—" Mrs. Gorman rubbed at her eyes. "You'll have to excuse me. When you knocked, I thought it was that man again, the one who came and asked me all the questions. What was your name, dear?"

"Monica."

"Yes, that's it. Monica. Did you come to see Rhoda? She's not here. She's with her mother."

"Have you—have you heard from her?"

"Heard from her? Oh, no. That child never writes."

"But do you *know* she's at her mother's?"

"Oh, yes. She kept saying that was where she was going, and I said, 'Go if you want to. Nothing's stopping you.' "

"When did she go?"

"Yesterday—or it might have been the day before. I can't stand this light. Why don't you come in, child?"

Monica followed the old woman into a room that was littered with books and papers. Every window was closed. The air was stale and sickening. Monica began to cough.

"Would you like a drink of water?" asked Mrs. Gorman.

"No, thank you." Monica was looking at a picture on the mantel, the picture of a pretty, smiling woman with a flower in her hair.

"That's Rhoda's mother," said Mrs. Gorman.

"That's Elaine. I can show you some better pictures." She dusted off an album and put it into Monica's hands.

Monica turned the pages. There were pictures of Rhoda's mother in a dozen different poses, then pictures of a dark-haired young man. He had a thin moustache and a cruel smile.

"That's Rhoda's father," said Mrs. Gorman. "He left when Rhoda was born. Just disappeared, and nobody ever saw him again."

She brought out another album. "This has pictures of Rhoda. You wouldn't think it, but she was a pretty baby. If you'd like to see—"

"I can't stay. I'll come back when Rhoda is here."

Monica escaped into the sunlight and the clean fresh air. She went home.

Mother told her, "The sheriff stopped by. He's been to see Mrs. Gorman, and he found out about Rhoda. She's in New York with her mother."

"How does he know that?"

"Mrs. Gorman told him."

"I've been to see Mrs. Gorman, too," said Monica. "She's in a fog. I don't know how the sheriff can believe what she says."

"I think we can trust him," said Mother.

The evening was long. They went to bed early, but Monica was still awake at midnight when the telephone rang.

She went to Mother's room. "Who was it?"

"The sheriff," answered Mother. "He just came from the haunted house. Everything was all right. He didn't see anyone."

"Why did he go over there?"

"Because of the note. It said to go there tonight, remember?"

"It said for *me* to go."

"Well, nobody was there, and Rhoda is safe in

New York, so we can all stop worrying, can't we? . . . Can't we, Monica?"

"What about the note?"

"The note?"

"Yes. Who wrote it?"

"We *don't* know that yet, do we?" said Mother. "But I think the sheriff will find out if we just give him time."

In the morning Monica started to school. She went down the walk, past the tent, nearly to the gate. There she stopped. There'd been something about the tent—something that hadn't quite belonged there. . . .

She went back. This time she saw clearly what was different—a small patch of brown against the blue of the tent. It was a piece of paper tucked into the flap. Another note.

These words were not made of cutout letters.

These were printed on the paper.

> *Monica. You have betrayed me. This is your last chance. Come to haunted house tonight. You can still save your friend. Come at midnight. Tell no one. Tell no one.*

Midnight

That day there were two Monicas. One was Monica-as-usual, going from class to class, playing volleyball, having lunch on the grass with Fran and Audrey. The other was Monica-with-a-secret, scared and excited, hot and cold, asking herself over and over, What will happen? What will happen now?

"You're awfully jumpy," said Fran on the way home.

"Jumpy?" said Monica.

"When anyone speaks to you, you sort of jump."

"You're keeping something from us," said Audrey.

They wanted to walk home with her. They wanted her to go over to the lake with them. She had a hard time getting away from them, but at last she was alone. She was at home in her room where she could think.

She took the note out of her lunch box and read it again for what clues she could find. It was printed on a scrap torn from a paper bag. The printing had been done with a pencil. The letters were neat and large, the kind of printing almost anyone might have done.

You have betrayed me. She knew what that meant, of course. She hadn't gone to the haunted house last night. The sheriff had gone instead.

This is your last chance . . . Come to haunted house tonight . . . You can still save your friend . . . Come at midnight . . . Tell no one . . .

She tried to picture whoever it was who had written the note, walked across the yard last night, and slipped it into the tent. Someone small and quick, who moved softly? A man? A woman? Someone she knew? Someone who knew her?

"Monica—?" Mother was at the door.

Monica put the note out of sight under her pillow.

But Mother didn't come in. "Dinner," she said, and went away.

They sat down to dinner. Chicken salad with white grapes. Sliced tomatoes. Iced tea. The kind of dinner Monica liked, but she couldn't eat.

"Not hungry?" asked Mother.

"Not yet."

"Maybe later. Everything will keep."

"Excuse me," said Monica. "I need to study my part in the play."

She studied her part. At ten o'clock she went out to say good night.

"Would you like your dinner now?" asked Mother.

"Thank you, I'm still not hungry."

Back in her room, she turned out the light and lay down. Her little clock ticked away on the table beside her. Its face glowed in the dark. She watched the time.

She didn't *have* to go to the haunted house. She could tell Mother about the note, and Mother could call the sheriff.

But he hadn't believed her before. Why should he believe her now? She wasn't even sure Mother would believe her.

You have betrayed me. This is your last chance . . . You can still save your friend . . . Tell no one . . .

She did have to go. She did. Somehow she had become the key. Everything depended on her.

It was 10:30. It was 11.

At a little past 11:30 she quietly left her room. Without turning on a light, she went down the hall to the back door. She let herself out of the house.

The night was clear, and there was a half-moon.

No cars passed as she walked along the road. There was no light at Mrs. Gorman's. She turned down the lane that led to the haunted house.

She could see the house. Its roof and chimney were dark above the trees ahead.

She pushed through the grass that had grown high in the lane. She came to the house. The door was open. Moonlight shone in and made a path across the floor.

It was midnight—she was here. What now?

Beside the house something moved.

A voice spoke. "This way."

The Old Garden

The voice was hollow and low. It could have been a man's or a woman's. It said again, "This way."

A figure seemed to float from the shadow of the house. It moved away, and she followed.

She went down three steps into the old garden. She knew the garden. Here was the path with the well on one side and rosebushes on the other. She waded through weeds and vines.

The figure had stopped. It was wrapped in something dark, and it wore a mask.

"Stay there," it said. "Are you alone?"

"Yes," said Monica.

"Did you tell?"

"No."

"Turn your back."

Monica turned. The voice was disguised. She tried to think where she had heard it before.

Steps came toward her. A piece of cloth—a blindfold—was pulled roughly over her eyes.

"No!" She ducked from under the cloth.

"Hold still!"

And now she knew where she had heard the voice before. She faced the figure. She caught at the mask—a paper bag with torn holes for eyes.

The paper ripped, and a face looked out at her. Rhoda's face.

They stood without moving. Rhoda was pale, her mouth drawn thin.

"You had to find out, didn't you?" she said.

"You weren't kidnapped," said Monica.

"Who said I was?"

"*You* wrote the notes. You've been hiding."

"Yes. Under your noses. Do you know where? Most of the time in my grandmother's attic."

"She said you were gone."

"She didn't know. She doesn't know anything. When the sheriff's car came and he flashed his light around last night, I was right over there." Rhoda pointed to the garden wall. "I thought if I tried one more note, I'd get you here, and I *did* get you here."

"Why?" asked Monica.

"Remember the game?"

"What game?"

"You know. On the way home from school. I tried to make you look at me, and you wouldn't. That's when I hid. I thought I'd make you worry, and I did, didn't I?"

"You mean this whole thing is just part of that silly game?"

"That's how it started. But while I was hiding, I thought what I *really* wanted to do—where I *really* wanted to see you." Rhoda's mouth jerked. "If you only knew how much I hate you!"

Monica felt as if she had been struck. Rhoda moved closer. "The very first day you shut the door in my face. I wasn't good enough for you. Not when you had Mother and Daddy and all your friends. You were Beauty and I was the Beast."

"Rhoda—"

"You could have anything you wanted without lifting a finger. You even won all the games, but you won't win this one!"

She had hold of Monica's arms. She was pushing her. It was like a slow, crazy dance.

Monica's ankle struck something. She looked back. She had come up against a round wooden circle—the cover of the old well. Just behind her was the well itself, a dark hole with a low stone curb. Rhoda was pushing her toward it.

Monica fought. She twisted almost free. Rhoda seized her again.

They wrestled on the edge of the well. Monica tripped on the well curb. She was falling. Her hand was wound in Rhoda's hair, and Rhoda was falling with her.

They landed in a heap at the bottom of the well. A shower of dirt and small stones fell from above. Then there was silence.

Monica tried to catch her breath. Rhoda was lying across her.

"Get off," she said.

Rhoda moved a little.

Monica straightened her arms and legs. She wasn't hurt. The well was not deep, and the bottom was soft with mud.

Overhead she could see a circle of sky with a few stars in it.

Rhoda was sobbing.

"You're not hurt," said Monica. "You fell mostly on me."

She stood up. Her shoes stuck in the mud. She felt the sides of the well, the damp earth and slippery stones. There were no footholds that she could find.

She thought of asking Rhoda, Do you have any matches? Do you have a flashlight?

It was all completely mad, something not to be believed. One minute they'd been fighting tooth and nail. The next, they were at the bottom of the well, with no one to turn to but each other!

Rhoda whimpered something. It sounded a little as if she had said, "I'm sorry."

"*Are* you sorry?" asked Monica.

"Yes!" said Rhoda.

"So am I," said Monica. "I'm sorry you thought you had to go through all this."

Rhoda hiccupped.

"And don't be sick!" Monica was still feeling the damp rough sides of the well. "I have an idea . . . Are you listening?"

"Yes," said Rhoda.

"If I could get on your shoulders—" said Monica. "Stand up."

Rhoda stood up.

"Bend over," said Monica. "Are you bending over? I'll get on your back and—"

"Stop," said Rhoda. "It hurts."

"Can you get on my back?" Monica knelt. "Here—see if you can. Stand on my shoulders . . . put your hands against the sides. Don't fall off."

Slowly she rose, wobbling under Rhoda's weight. Then the weight was gone. She could hear Rhoda scrambling out of the well.

Monica waited. "Pull me up," she shouted. "Reach down with a stick or a vine or something. Can you hear me?"

There was the sound of laughter. Rhoda's voice came faintly down to her, "Last look!"

The circle of sky was gone. The cover had been dragged back over the well.

The New Girl

Monica stood there, trying to think, trying to understand. She could believe that Rhoda hated her, had plotted to bring her here and push her into the well. But then they'd been in the well together. Rhoda had said she was sorry. They'd had to depend on each other.

Surely Rhoda wouldn't go away and leave her. Not now.

But Rhoda *had* gone. She'd dragged the cover over the well and left her. . . .

Monica wondered how soon she would be missed

at home. Probably not until breakfast time. And how long would it be until someone found her? It might be hours—or days.

She shouted a few times, but the well seemed to swallow the sound of her voice.

It wasn't far to the top. If she could dig steps up the side of the well—

She found a flat stone and began to dig and scrape with it. She could make hardly a dent in the rocky wall, but she worked until she was tired. Her knees bent. She knelt like a frog in the mud at the bottom of the well.

She tried to count the seconds and minutes. It was something to do.

Then she was listening. A sound had come from overhead. There was a light. It shone into the well, blinding her. She heard a voice.

"Rhoda," she said.

But it wasn't Rhoda. It was the sheriff.

He had taken off his jacket and was holding it

down to her. She caught hold of the sleeve, and he pulled her out.

Mother was there with a flashlight in her hand. She dropped it and reached for Monica.

"Are you all right?"

"No," said Monica. "I'm all muddy."

Mother began to laugh, and Monica laughed, too. They couldn't stop.

"That's enough," said the sheriff. "You can stop the hysterics."

They stopped.

He picked up the flashlight. He was leading them out of the garden.

Monica asked, "How did you find me?"

"You hadn't been yourself all evening," Mother said. "I went to your room to see how you were, and you were gone. I found the note in your bed, so I called the sheriff. We came here, and he caught Rhoda running out of the garden."

"And she told you where I was?"

"Not at first. She said she didn't know."

"We took her to the station," said the sheriff. "Her mother was there—"

"Her *mother?*" said Monica.

"Yes. I kept thinking maybe the girl hadn't gone to New York after all. I tried to get her mother on the telephone, and finally I got through to her. She didn't have any idea where the girl was. She came right up from New York."

"When Rhoda saw her, she broke down and told everything," said Mother. "It was the strangest story I ever heard."

"Why did she hate me so?" asked Monica.

"She probably didn't hate you as much as she hated herself," said Mother. "And she didn't mean to leave you in the well forever. She was going to let you out after a while. But she had some twisted idea of getting revenge."

"Revenge for what?" asked Monica.

"It's hard to put it all together," said Mother.

"She talked about how life had always been against her. She came here to get a new start, and she thought you'd kept her from it."

"Is that—is that what she said?" asked Monica.

"It was something like that," said Mother. "I tried to tell her how you'd gone out of your way to be good to her and make her welcome—"

"Mother," said Monica.

"What?"

"I didn't know she needed help. If I'd known, I wouldn't have shut her out."

"But you didn't shut her out. From the first you were good to her. You made her welcome—"

"I wasn't good to her."

"Of course you were," said Mother.

"I wasn't!" Monica heard her own voice rising higher. "I never was *really* good to her. I—I shut the door!"

The sheriff was saying, "It's been a bad shock for her. Let's get her home."

He picked her up and carried her. With her face against his shoulder, she closed her eyes and grew quiet.

All the next day she stayed at home. There were telephone calls from Madame Vere, from Fran and Audrey, from some of the other girls at school. They missed her, they said. They hoped she would soon be back.

"Do they know?" asked Monica.

"They know part of it," said Mother. "Not all."

"I don't want to talk about it."

"You don't have to. Not till you're ready."

Monica said, "Maybe I'll go back to school to-morrow."

"Are you sure you're ready?"

"I have to go back sometime," said Monica. "There's no use waiting."

She went to school the next morning. She walked

with Fran and Audrey. They asked no questions. She was sure they had been told not to. They were watching her, and she felt strange with them. She almost wished she were alone.

They went into the study hall. Madame was at her desk.

"Since we're all a bit early," she said, "I'll tell you the news now. One of our girls has left us. Rhoda has gone back to New York to live with her mother. And" —Madame smiled— "we have a new girl."

Monica looked toward Rhoda's old place. The new girl was there.

"She lives on South Beach, and she is here for the summer," said Madame. "Will you please stand, Martha?"

The girl stood. Her face was small and serious. She made a quick little bow. Just before she sat down, her eyes met Monica's.

She may be my best friend, thought Monica. She may be my worst enemy. She may not be anything much to me, or she may be more than I can imagine. Whatever she is, I don't know now. I'll have to wait to know. And while I wait, I won't close the door. This time I'll try to keep it open.